THIS WALKER BOOK BELONGS TO:

Conisbron Nursery

For Marje, Pat and Grace, librarians and friends
D. M.

For Jacob, Jesse and Elieanna – great kids with bellybuttons
R. C.

First published 2005 by Walker Books Ltd
87 Vauxhall Walk, London SE11 5HJ

4 6 8 10 9 7 5

Text © 2005 David Martin
Illustrations © 2005 Randy Cecil

The right of David Martin and Randy Cecil to be identified as author
and illustrator respectively of this work has been asserted by them
in accordance with the Copyright, Designs and Patents Act 1988

This book has been typeset in Clichee and Helvetica Bold

Printed in China

British Library Cataloguing in Publication Data:
a catalogue record for this book
is available from the British Library

ISBN-13: 978-0-7445-9320-4
ISBN-10: 0-7445-9320-4

www.walkerbooks.co.uk

We've All Got Bellybuttons!

David Martin

illustrated by Randy Cecil

WALKER BOOKS

AND SUBSIDIARIES

LONDON · BOSTON · SYDNEY · AUCKLAND

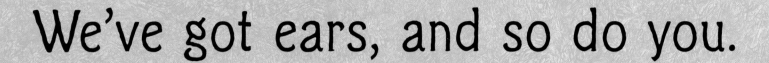

We've got ears, and so do you.

We can pull them.

Can you?

We've got hands, and so do you.
We can clap them.

Can you?

We've got necks, and so do you.

We can stretch them.

We've got feet, and so do you.

We can kick them.

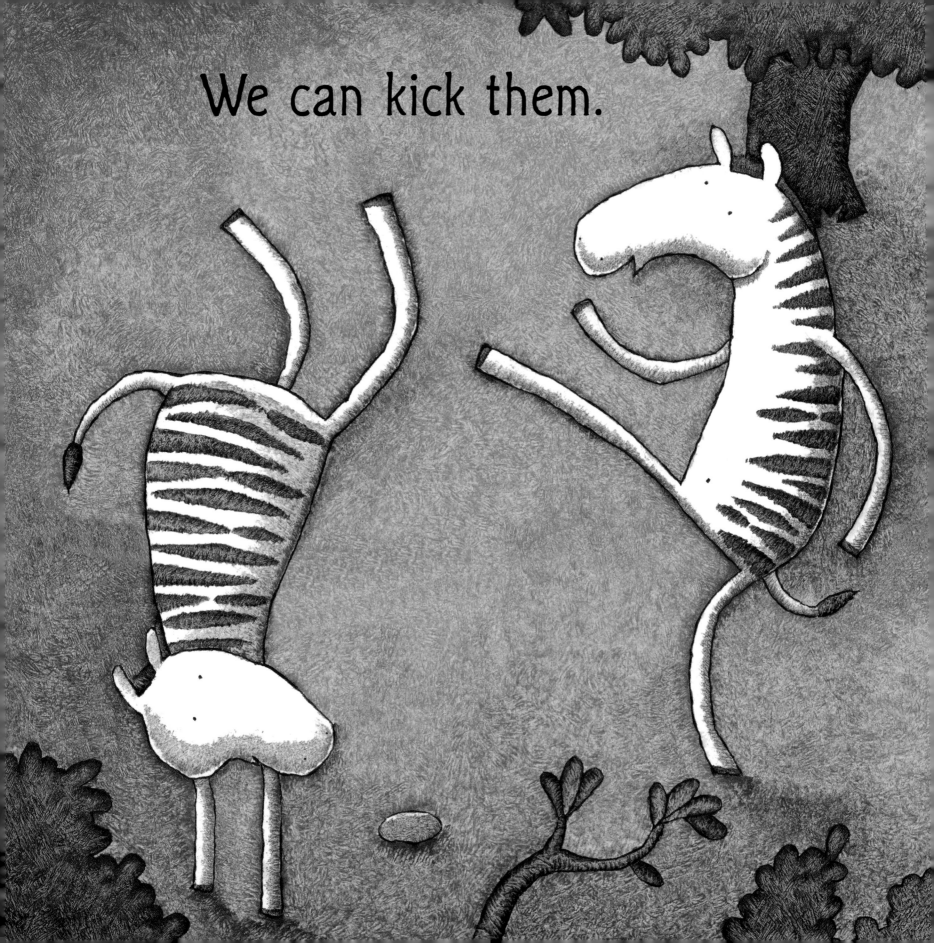

Can you?

We've got eyes,
and so do you.

We can close them.

Can you?

We've got mouths, and so do you.

And we've all got bellybuttons,

and so do you.

And when they're tickle, tickle,

tickled ...

we GIGGLE!

Do you?